This book belongs to:

Anne Isaacs

PANCAKES for SUPPER!

Illustrated by
Mark Teague

SCHOLASTIC INC.
New York Toronto London Auckland Sydney
Mexico City New Delhi Hong Kong Buenos Aires

For Dianne Hess, editor and friend, with love — A. I.

For Jean Feiwel, my friend and mentor — M. T.

Once upon a morning in a March wood,

a solitary wagon splashed along the mud road toward
the town of Whisker Creek. Winter was almost gone, but it
had left snowy footprints on the land. Mama and Papa guided
the horses, while Toby sat in the back and made up a song to
the rhythm of the bouncing wagon.

I've got a sky-blue coat with purple lining,
A sun-yellow sweater with green leaves twining,
Thick orange mittens with a matching cap,
Buck hide boots to keep out the damp,
Fuzzy red long johns and a dress of brown:
Brand-new clothes for Whisker Creek town!

Suddenly the wagon hit a BIG BUMP and sent Toby flying!

Up she sailed, higher and higher and higher, past squirrels in the branches, past soaring eagles and feathery clouds, until she could no longer see her parents' wagon.

Then, just as Toby was wondering if she would ever come down again, she began to fall.

Down, down, down she tumbled, until finally she landed—*SPLOOSH*—in a deep, soft pile of snow.

But right in front of her stood a huge wolf with terrible green eyes! The wolf paced around Toby in a circle, closer and closer.

"*HUNGR-R-R-Y*," growled the wolf.
"So hungry am I,
I will feast on the child
Who falls from the sky!"

"Oh! Please don't eat me," cried Toby, "and I will make you the grandest animal in the forest!"

"A small girl like you?

Ha! What can *you* do?" growled the wolf.

"I will give you my beautiful blue coat with purple lining."

The wolf's eyes gleamed fiercely as it put on Toby's coat and strutted off, calling:

"Now *I'm* the grandest beast,
West or East!"

Toby ran off as fast as she could, but just as she reached the crest of a hill, she found herself face to face with a cougar!

"*RAAAR-R-R*!" the cougar roared.

"Kits in the den, waiting to eat!

My kitties would love a girl so sweet!"

"Oh! Please don't eat me," Toby cried as the cougar crouched to spring, "and I will make you the grandest animal in the forest."

"A small girl like you?
Ha! What can *you* do?"
roared the cougar.

"I will give you my beautiful yellow sweater,"
said Toby.

The cougar gloated triumphantly as it strutted
off in Toby's sweater, roaring:
"Now *I'm* the grandest beast,
West or East."

Toby shivered without her warm coat and sweater, and peered fearfully into the woods as she ran on. How would she ever find her parents now? In her hurry, Toby didn't notice a furry, white-striped animal crawling through the shadows. But it noticed *her*, for just then she heard a whispered snarl:

"Come to play?
Go away!
Plan to stay?
Go away. Go away!
Or I'll *SP—SP—*SPRAY!"
Toby backed off as quickly as she could, but the skunk was already raising its tail, aiming straight at her!

"Oh, please don't spray me," cried Toby, "and I will make you the grandest animal in the forest."

"A *psssmall* girl like you?

P*shaw*! What can **you** do?"

snarled the skunk.

"I will give you my beautiful buck hide boots," said Toby. The skunk waddled over to put the boots on its muddy front paws and strutted away, whispering:

"Now **I'm** the grandest beast,

West or Ea**sss-s**t!"

Toby ran off holding her nose, until suddenly . . .

. . . a porcupine jumped right in front of her, threatening
her with its long, sharp quills!

"Approach me if you dare—
But beware!
If you try to pull my hair—
Beware!
You haven't got a prayer
If you touch me anywhere—
So beware!"

"Oh! Don't strike me with your quills," cried Toby, "and I will make you the grandest animal in the forest."

"A small girl like you?

Ha! What can **you** do?"

"I will give you my beautiful brown dress," said Toby.

A minute later, the porcupine shambled off wearing Toby's dress, bristling with pride and crying:

"Now **I'm** the grandest beast,

West or East!"

Now the only clothes Toby had on were her red long johns, her orange mittens, and her hat. She had just sat down to rub her frozen toes when a fierce growl arose behind her. There stood a bear, half as tall as a tree, and it drooled hungrily as it grunted:

"Girl for dinner! Crunchy! Good!
Roasted on a stack of wood—
Or should I stew her? Yes, I should!

Young, but ripe enough to eat!
Crunchy fingers! Crunchy feet!
Dipped in honey—very sweet!"

"Oh! Please don't eat me, and I will make you the grandest animal in the forest," cried Toby.

"What can *you* do,
Little Tasty-in-Stew?"

"I will give you my beautiful orange mittens," said Toby, but the bear only laughed and came closer.

"What good would that do?
I've got four paws, not two."

Toby thought fast. "You can wear them on your ears," she told the bear.

A minute later the bear lumbered off, wearing Toby's mittens on its ears and thundering:

"Now *I'm* the grandest beast,
West or East!"

Toby hurried off, rubbing her cold fingers, but she hadn't gone far when she heard a tremendou uproar. *Oh, no!* thought Toby. ***The animals are al coming back to eat me!*** And she scurried up the nearest tree to hide.

Soon the wolf, cougar, skunk, porcupine, and bear appeared,
roaring and growling,
hissing and howling,
yipping and yowling,
and arguing over which of them was the grandest.

The animals grew so angry that they began to chase each other. All their fine new clothes fell off as they ran. They caught hold of each other's tails and raced around the trunk of a huge maple tree. Soon they were spinning so fast that Toby couldn't tell which animal was which. Round and round the animals whirled, faster and faster, until at last they melted into a great golden-brown puddle at the base of the trunk.

As soon as she was sure the animals were gone for good, Toby ran to put on her clothes. Then she heard her mother and father calling her, and caught sight of their wagon through the trees. Everyone shouted joyfully as Toby ran out to meet them.

While Toby told them of her adventures, the sun rose high and warmed the trunk of the maple tree where the animals had disappeared. The tree began to stir with life after its long winter sleep, and soaked up the golden-brown puddle from root to branch. A woodpecker tapped holes in the bark and sweet maple syrup began to trickle down.

"Pancakes for supper!" shouted Toby, and she held a shiny tin bucket to collect the syrup.

"We'll have the grandest feast, West or East!" said Papa, and he built a fire in a clearing, while Mama mixed batter in a bowl.

Mama fried pancakes as golden as the fur on a cougar, while the hot maple syrup Toby poured over them was as glossy-brown as a bear's coat. (But not one single pancake was as tough as a wolf, prickly as a porcupine, or smelly as a skunk!)

Papa ate twenty-seven pancakes, and Mama ate fifty-five, but Toby ate one hundred and sixty-nine, because she was so hungry.

"For you're the bravest girl in the world!" said Mama and Papa together . . .

. . . and Toby drove the horses
all the way to Whisker Creek.

ISBN-13: 978-0-439-93091-8
ISBN-10: 0-439-93091-X

12 11 10 9 8 7 6 5 4 3 2 1   7 8 9 10 11 12/0

Printed in Singapore   46

This edition first printing, March 2007

The artwork was created in oil on paper.
The text was set in NeutraText.
Book design by Rich Deas.

Pancakes for Supper! is based on *The Story of Little Black Sambo*,
written by Helen Bannerman and first published in 1899.
Setting the present story in New England, Anne Isaacs blends elements from
American storytelling traditions and Bannerman's tale, while
introducing animals indigenous to North America
and an indomitable new heroine.